The Books About Josefina

Meet Josefina · An American Girl

Josefina and her sisters are struggling after Mamá's death, when a surprise gives Josefina hope—and a wonderful idea.

Josefina Learns a Lesson · A School Story

Tía Dolores brings exciting changes for Josefina and her sisters. But will all the changes make them forget Mamá?

❀

Josefina's Surprise · A Christmas Story

A very special Christmas celebration helps heal Josefina and her family.

Also available in Spanish

JOSEFINA'S
SURPRISE
A CHRISTMAS STORY
BY VALERIE TRIPP
ILLUSTRATIONS JEAN-PAUL TIBBLES
VIGNETTES SUSAN MCALILEY

PLEASANT COMPANY

Published by Pleasant Company Publications
© Copyright 1997 by Pleasant Company
For information, address: Book Editor, Pleasant Company Publications,
8400 Fairway Place, P.O. Box 620998, Middleton, WI 53562.

First Edition.
Printed in the United States of America.
97 98 99 00 01 02 RND 10 9 8 7 6 5 4 3 2 1

The American Girls Collection®, Josefina™, and Josefina Montoya™
are trademarks of Pleasant Company.

PERMISSIONS & PICTURE CREDITS
Grateful acknowledgment is made to María Elba C De Baca, Las Vegas, NM, for permission
to quote the verses appearing on pp. 42, 45, and 57, originally published in the booklet
The Christmas Season by Elba C De Baca.

The following individuals and organizations have generously given permission to reprint
illustrations contained in "Looking Back": pp. 62-63—Jack Parsons Photography, Santa Fe, NM
(church); gift of the Historical Society of New Mexico to the Museum of International Folk Art,
Museum of New Mexico, Santa Fe, accession #A.5.59-3, Blair Clark photo (Nativity scene);
© 1997 Douglas Merriam, Santa Fe (turnovers and tamales); pp. 64-65—*Fandango* by Theodore
Gentilz, courtesy Daughters of the Republic of Texas Library at the Alamo; Collections of the
Museum of International Folk Art, Museum of New Mexico, and Spanish Colonial Arts Society,
Santa Fe (chocolate pot, cup, stirrer); Palace of the Governors collections, Museum of New
Mexico, Santa Fe (fiddle); courtesy of the Institute of Texan Cultures, University of Texas, San
Antonio (angel); photo by Aaron B. Craycraft, courtesy of the Museum of New Mexico, Santa Fe,
neg. #13695 (*Los Pastores* play); pp. 66-67—Jack Parsons Photography, Santa Fe (Deer Dance);
Spanish Colonial Arts Society, Santa Fe, accession #PR.68.46, photo by Jack Parsons Photography
(three kings); History Collections, Los Angeles County Museum of Natural History (shoes);
©1994 George Ancona (girl on burro); Jack Parsons Photography, Santa Fe (farolitos).

Edited by Peg Ross and Judith Woodburn
Designed by Mark Macauley, Myland McRevey, Laura Moberly, and Jane S. Varda
Art Directed by Jane S. Varda

Library of Congress Cataloging-in-Publication Data

Tripp, Valerie, 1951-
Josefina's surprise : a Christmas story / by Valerie Tripp ;
illustrations Jean-Paul Tibbles ; vignettes Susan McAliley. — 1st ed.
  p. cm. — (The American girls collection)
"Book three"—P. [1] of cover.
Summary: The second Christmas after their mother has died, Josefina and her three sisters
find that participating in the traditions of Las Posadas helps keep memories of Mamá alive.
ISBN 1-56247-520-7 (hardcover). — ISBN 1-56247-519-3 (pbk)
[1. Posadas (Social custom)—Fiction. 2. Christmas—Fiction. 3. Mexican Americans—Fiction.
4. Sisters—Fiction. 5. New Mexico—History—To 1848—Fiction.]
I. Tibbles, Jean-Paul, ill. II. Title. III. Series.
PZ7.T7363Jr 1997 [Fic]—dc21 97-11826 CIP AC

TO GRANGER WILLIAM TRIPP
AND PAIGE ELIZABETH TRIPP
WITH LOVE

Josefina and her family speak Spanish, so you'll see some Spanish words in this book. If you can't tell what a word means from reading the story or looking at the illustrations, you can turn to the "Glossary of Spanish Words" that begins on page 68. It will tell you what the word means and how to pronounce it.

Remember that in Spanish, "j" is pronounced like "h." That means Josefina's name is pronounced "ho-seh-FEE-nah."

TABLE OF CONTENTS

Josefina's Family

Papá
Josefina's father, who guides his family and his rancho with quiet strength.

Ana
Josefina's oldest sister, who is married and has two little boys.

Josefina
A nine-year-old girl whose heart and hopes are as big as the New Mexico sky.

Francisca
Josefina's fifteen-year-old sister, who is headstrong and impatient.

Clara
Josefina's practical, sensible sister, who is twelve years old.

TÍA DOLORES
*Josefina's aunt, who
has lived far away in
Mexico City for ten years.*

TERESITA
*Tía Dolores's servant,
an excellent weaver.*

CHRISTMAS IS COMING

The wind was playing with Josefina.
First it made her skirt billow out behind
her and the ends of her *rebozo* fly up
like wings. Then it swirled around and pushed
against her back, hurrying her along like a helpful
but impatient hand. Josefina smiled. She could see
that the wind was playing with her sisters and Tía
Dolores, too. They looked like birds with ruffled
feathers as they were blown along the road on this
blustery morning.

Josefina, her three sisters, and Tía Dolores were
on their way to the village about a mile from their
rancho. The road ran between the stream and the
fields and under tall cottonwood trees. The trees

were bare now. The windswept fields were a wintry, stubbly brown. It was December. Christmas was coming, and today everyone was gathering to clean the church so that it would be ready to decorate. Josefina's papá had gone ahead with a burro loaded with wood for Christmas bonfires. The sisters and Tía Dolores would join him and their friends and neighbors at the church.

"Oh!" exclaimed Francisca, exasperated. The wind was blowing her hair so that it curled wildly around her face. Francisca was Josefina's second-oldest sister. She was very careful about how she looked, especially when she was going to the village. She pulled her rebozo up over her head and tried to hold it in place with one hand as she struggled to carry a basket in her other hand.

Josefina didn't care if her hair was windblown. She slipped her arm under Francisca's basket. "I'll carry this," she said.

"*Gracias,*" said Francisca. She let go of the basket and held her rebozo tightly under her chin with both hands.

Josefina glanced at the bright red chiles in the basket. "Why are you bringing these?" she asked Francisca.

"They're for Señora Sánchez," said Francisca.

"Don't you remember, Josefina?" asked Ana, the oldest sister. "Mamá always gave Señora Sánchez some of our chiles at this time of year. Señora Sánchez claimed she couldn't make her traditional stew without them."

"Oh, that's right," said Josefina. "I remember."

Tía Dolores smiled at Josefina. "I'm eager to taste Señora Sánchez's famous stew," she said. "I'm glad Christmas is coming soon."

Josefina could only manage a very small smile in return. She saw that Clara, her next oldest sister, was frowning. Ana and Francisca didn't look very enthusiastic, either.

Tía Dolores looked at the sisters' faces. "What's the matter?" she asked.

Ana answered. "When Mamá was alive, Christmas was always happy," she said. "But last Christmas came soon after Mamá's death. All we could think of was how much we missed her."

Tía Dolores spoke quietly. "It must have been very hard," she said.

Josefina slid her hand into Tía Dolores's. She knew that last Christmas must have been hard for her, too. Tía Dolores had been far away in Mexico City when Mamá died. How sad and lonely she must have been! Tía Dolores was Mamá's sister, and she missed Mamá as much as Josefina, Clara, Francisca, and Ana did. A few months ago, Tía Dolores had come to stay on the rancho to help Josefina's family, and for that Josefina was grateful every single day.

"Last year, Christmas was very quiet," said Francisca. "There were no parties or dances, out of respect for Mamá. No one felt like celebrating anyway."

For a while the sisters and Tía Dolores walked without talking. They were all remembering last year and wondering what this Christmas would be like. Josefina listened to the stream as it splashed over rocks and around curves. The stream flowed steadily and cheerfully. Josefina wished she could be as carefree about the holiday that lay ahead.

She asked Tía Dolores about one thing that was worrying her. "Would it be *wrong* to be happy this

Christmas?" she said. "Would it be disrespectful
to Mamá?"

"No, I don't think so," said Tía Dolores. "The
year of mourning has passed. Christmas is a blessed
time. I'm sure God means for us to be happy, and
to celebrate the birth of His son, Jesús." She looked
down at Josefina. "And I'm sure your mamá would
want you to be happy. She'd want you to pray and
sing and celebrate with your friends and neighbors."

"*Sí,*"Ana agreed. "Mamá would want us to
follow all the Christmas traditions."

"I think so, too," said Francisca.

"Well," Clara said flatly. "We may follow the
traditions, but they won't be the same without
Mamá."

Somewhere inside Josefina a knot tightened.
Clara is right, she thought.

"Mamá loved Christmas traditions," Josefina
said to Tía Dolores. "She even started a new one in
our family. Every Christmas, she'd make a doll dress
for—"

"Oh, Josefina!" exclaimed Ana, interrupting.
"You're talking about Niña, aren't you? Niña should
have been given to you last Christmas."

"But she never was," said Josefina.

Tía Dolores looked puzzled. "Who's Niña?" she asked.

Ana explained, "When I was eight, Mamá made a doll for me. She named the doll Niña. Every Christmas, Mamá made a new dress for Niña. Then, the year Francisca was eight, I gave Niña to her."

"Sí," said Francisca. "And the Christmas when Clara was eight, I gave Niña to *her*."

"Of course, last year Mamá was not here to make a dress for Niña," said Ana sadly. She turned to Clara. "But you could have given Niña to Josefina anyway, Clara. What happened?"

Josefina was curious to hear Clara's answer.

But Clara only shrugged and said, "I guess I forgot."

"Never mind, Clara," said Tía Dolores. "You can give the doll to Josefina this Christmas. I'll help you make a new dress for her. Where is Niña? I've never seen her."

"I haven't seen her in a long time, either," said Francisca.

"Neither have I," said Josefina, looking at Clara.

"Oh, she's around somewhere," said Clara. Her

voice sounded unworried, but just for a second, a troubled look clouded her eyes. The look came and went so quickly, Josefina thought she must have imagined it.

Francisca, who was messy, liked to tease Clara, who was neat. "Heavens!" she said. "Do you mean to say that you've *lost* Niña?"

"She's not lost," said Clara crossly, kicking a pebble with her shoe. "I told you. She's around somewhere. I'll look for her when I have time."

"Would you like me to help you look?" Josefina asked. She didn't want to make Clara more cross, but she really did want Niña. "Christmas is coming soon, and—"

"I know!" said Clara sharply. "I don't need any help! I'll find her!"

"Of course you will, Clara," said Tía Dolores.

Tía Dolores sounded so sure that Clara would find Niña. Josefina wished *she* could be as sure. How could Clara possibly have misplaced something as precious as Niña? Where could the doll be?

At that moment, Josefina made up her mind. She was going to look for Niña herself, no matter what Clara said. After all, Niña was *supposed* to be hers.

Josefina's decision to look for Niña cheered her.
She couldn't help feeling a little hopeful, just as
she couldn't help feeling a little excited because
she heard music. Josefina quickened her steps.
The music was faint but clear, floating up from
the village.

"Listen!" said Tía Dolores.

They all lifted their faces and listened. The
music grew louder and stronger. It seemed to urge
them, *Come along! Come along!* Soon they were
all walking so fast they were practically dancing.
Josefina's thick braid bounced against her back,
and even sensible Clara skipped a little bit. The
sound of the music mixed in the air with the spicy
scent of burning *piñón* wood. As they came to the
village, they saw smoke rising up from chimneys
into the cloudless blue sky.

It was a small village. Josefina
knew everyone in all of the twelve
families who lived there. She knew
their houses, too, which were built
close together and seemed to lean toward
each other like old friends. The houses were made
of earth-colored *adobe.* They were surrounded by

hard-packed dirt, fenced pens for the animals, and vegetable gardens now sleeping under bumpy winter blankets of brown dirt. Most of the houses faced the clean-swept *plaza* at the center of the village. The biggest and most important building in the village was the church. It was one story tall except for the front, where the bell was hung high above the doors.

Today, the doors of the church were wide open. People scurried in and out carrying brooms and brushes, tools, and scrubbing rags. They hauled big, sloshing tubs of water up from the stream.

"Buenos días! It's good to see you! How are you today?" everyone called out when they saw Tía Dolores and the sisters.

"Buenos días! We're very well, thank you," they called back over the sound of the music and the noise of dogs barking and hammers pounding. People were talking, and every once in a while Josefina would hear swoops of laughter from the little children as they chased one another.

Clara, Francisca, and Ana went inside the church to start working. But Tía Dolores and Josefina lingered outside next to the musicians.

One man was playing a guitar, and two others were playing violins. As Josefina and Tía Dolores listened, the music changed. The men began to play a slow, sweet song. All the noise and conversation seemed to fade away for Josefina. All she could hear was the music.

"I haven't heard this lullaby since I was a child," said Tía Dolores. She hummed along with the music for a moment, and then she asked Josefina, "Please, will you sing it for me?"

Josefina nodded. Very softly, she began to sing:

> *Sleep my beautiful baby,*
> *Sleep my grain of gold.*
> *The night is very cold,*
> *The night is . . .*

Josefina's throat tightened, and she couldn't finish the song. She turned her head away and looked down at the basket of chiles she was carrying so that Tía Dolores wouldn't see that her eyes had filled with tears.

But Tía Dolores had seen them already. She put her hand under Josefina's chin and gently turned Josefina's face toward her.

All the noise and conversation seemed to fade away for Josefina.
All she could hear was the music.

"Mamá used to sing that lullaby to me when I was little," said Josefina. "And we always sang it together at church on Christmas Eve to baby Jesús."

Tía Dolores used the soft edge of her sleeve to dry Josefina's cheek. Then she asked, "Does everyone sing it?"

"Everyone sings the end," said Josefina. "But not the first part. That's sung alone by the girl who is María in *Las Posadas.*"

"You know," said Tía Dolores. "You're old enough to be María."

"Oh, I couldn't!" said Josefina. Her heart pounded faster at the very thought! Las Posadas was one of the most important and holy Christmas traditions. For nine nights in a row, everyone in the village acted out the story of the first Christmas Eve, when María and José were searching for shelter before baby Jesús was born. A girl took the role of María, riding a burro just as Jesús' mother did, and a man took the role of José. María and José and their followers went from house to house asking for shelter. Again and again they were turned away, until finally they were welcomed into the last house. On Christmas Eve, the final night of Las Posadas,

12

everyone was welcomed into the church instead of a house, and then Midnight Mass began.

"Sometimes," said Tía Dolores thoughtfully, "a girl wants to be María because she wants to pray for something special. I wonder what your prayer would be, Josefina, if you were María?"

Josefina did not have to wonder. She knew what her prayer would be. "I'd pray that this will be a happy Christmas," said Josefina, "for us and for Mamá in heaven."

Tía Dolores smiled. "That's a good prayer," she said. "Are you sure you don't want to be María?"

Josefina listened to the last notes of the lullaby. Part of her wanted to be María, but part of her knew she couldn't do it. "Last year, I could hardly sing the songs in Las Posadas," she said. "They made me so sad, because they reminded me that Mamá was gone. I'm afraid it'll be the same this year." She shook her head. "I couldn't possibly be María."

"I understand," said Tía Dolores. "It's still too soon for you." She tucked a strand of Josefina's hair behind her ear. "Let's go in now."

Josefina nodded, and walked into the church with Tía Dolores.

The church was usually a quiet, solemn place, and dim because the windows were very small and set deep in the thick walls. But today it was busy and noisy. Light poured in from the open doors and peeked through gaps in the roof where it had been damaged in a storm that fall.

Everywhere Josefina looked, she saw friends and neighbors and workers from Papá's rancho who'd put aside their usual chores to come and clean the church. Señora Sánchez, Señora López, and several other women chatted together as they swept. Josefina saw Papá's sister, Tía Magdalena, with a group of women who were polishing candlesticks. Ana, Francisca, and Clara were in a group of girls who were dusting. Boys, who were supposed to be scattering water over the floor to settle the dust, were splashing each other. Most of the men of the village stood together, their arms crossed over their chests, looking up at the roof and discussing the damage caused by the storm in the fall.

Josefina saw Papá standing with the men. Then Papá excused himself. "There you are!" he said to Josefina and Tía Dolores. "I was looking for you."

"We stopped outside to listen to the music," Tía Dolores explained.

"I might have known!" Papá said. His eyes twinkled. "You two are the musicians in our family."

Josefina could tell that Papá's compliment pleased Tía Dolores because she blushed a little. "Well," she said, "we're ready to work now!"

"Good," said Papá. He caught the eye of Señor García, who came over.

Señor García was the *mayordomo.* It was his job to assign tasks, because he and his wife took care of the church. Señor García was an old man, thin and stooped, with very white hair. He had a husky voice and stately manners. Everyone respected him for his knowledge and liked him for his kindness.

"God bless you!" Señor García said to Tía Dolores and Josefina. "I'm glad to see you. We need good willing hands like yours to help! I'm afraid the storm has made our work harder than usual. The roof caused terrible damage when it fell in. We have a lot to do before the priest comes on Christmas Eve. Will you two help with the sweeping?"

"We'd be glad to," said Tía Dolores.

"Gracias," said Señor García. Then he turned to

Papá. "May I ask your family to wash and iron the altar cloth, as you have done for many years?"

"Of course," said Papá.

"I remember when your dear wife gave that cloth to the church," said Señor García. "She'll be in our prayers this Christmas, I'm sure."

"Sí," said Papá quietly.

Señor García turned to Josefina again. "Josefina," he said. "I was wondering if you would like to be María in Las Posadas this Christmas, perhaps to offer a special prayer for your mamá?"

Josefina froze. Papá looked at her, waiting to hear her answer.

Tía Dolores put her arm around Josefina's shoulders. "It's very kind of you to ask, Señor García," she said. "But I think not this year."

"Ah, I see, I see," said Señor García gently. "Perhaps next year . . . Well, well, Margarita Sánchez can be María this Christmas."

Josefina didn't say anything. Just for a moment she leaned into Tía Dolores's arm, grateful for her understanding. Then she went to find Señora Sánchez to give her the basket of chiles.

The morning flew by so fast that Josefina was surprised when Señor García called everyone together for the closing prayer. "May God accept our work here today as a prayer of thanks for His merciful love," he said.

"Amen," said everyone together.

Josefina said her good-byes and walked out into the sunshine with her family. She had enjoyed sweeping and listening to the singsong of the women's voices as they gossiped and chattered around her. It had been nice to be part of the friendly group all scrubbing and sweeping and dusting together. Because of their work, the church shone. But now Josefina headed home with eager steps. She was determined to begin looking for Niña that very afternoon.

WHERE IS NIÑA?

Josefina closed her eyes and tried to picture Niña. The last time Josefina had seen her, Niña was wearing a pale blue skirt. Her arms and legs were flat because some of her stuffing had fallen out, and her black yarn hair was tangled. Josefina clearly remembered Niña's lively black eyes and smiling pink mouth, and she was pretty sure she remembered a green sash tied around Niña's waist. *I'll just keep my eyes sharp for any bit of green or black or pale blue,* Josefina thought. *Niña has to be somewhere.*

The first place Josefina looked was in the room she shared with Clara and Francisca. Standing on tiptoe, Josefina ran her hand along all the high shelves built into the walls. She looked in corners, under blankets, and behind the trunk that Clara and Francisca kept their clothes in. No Niña.

Josefina opened the trunk to search inside. Clara's clothes were folded neatly and stacked in precise piles. Josefina looked between them and under them but saw nothing. Francisca's clothes were loosely folded and piled in the trunk in such a haphazard way that Josefina had to dig through them. She did find a missing stocking, a broken button, and a hair ribbon that Francisca had loudly complained about losing. But she didn't find Niña.

Josefina sat back on her heels and sighed. *Where is Niña?* she wondered.

It was a question she asked herself hundreds of times a day as Christmas came nearer. No matter where she was or what else she was doing, Josefina was looking for Niña. She'd start searching early in the morning when the snow on the mountains still had its cool blue glow, and she wouldn't stop until late in the afternoon when sunset made the snow look rosy.

Josefina's eyes searched the *sala* when she knelt

there first thing in the morning for prayers with her family. Every time she walked to the stream to fetch water for the day, she looked around, hoping to see Niña hiding behind a rock or nestled at the foot of a tree. She explored every nook and cranny of the storerooms, the stables, and the chicken coops as she did her daily chores. She looked in the kitchen while

she made *bizcochito* cookies and in the courtyard while she waited for bread to bake. She looked in the cradle when she rocked Ana's baby son to sleep. She looked in the weaving room behind the

bizcochitos

looms, in the stacks of finished blankets, and in baskets full of wool waiting to be carded and spun. Still no Niña.

In desperation, Josefina even searched the goats' pen. "You haven't eaten Niña, have you?" she asked her old enemy, Florecita. The yellow-eyed goat looked at Josefina, blinked once, and turned away.

Josefina tried hard not to be discouraged, even though she soon felt as if she'd searched every inch of the rancho. Then one day, Josefina and her sisters and Tía Dolores were invited to Señora Sánchez's house. Josefina was glad to go. She knew that Clara

and Margarita Sánchez used to play dolls together. Maybe *that's* where Niña was. At least it was a new place to look!

"Buenos días! Please come in!" said Señora Sánchez as she welcomed everyone to her house. Almost all of the women and children from the village were there. The women had brought with them scraps of cloth and paper. They were using them to make flowers for *ramilletes* to decorate the church on Christmas Eve. Tía Dolores had brought some yellow material that was left over from the new dress Josefina had made for herself.

Señora Sánchez was a stout, good-hearted woman who was well known for being generous and neighborly. She'd been a special friend of Mamá's. They used to visit back and forth to share food and news and advice. Señora Sánchez always had time to sit and talk. And yet she seemed always to have something delicious cooking on the hearth, and her house was as neat as a pin. Mamá used to say she didn't know how Señora Sánchez did it!

But Señora Sánchez's house wasn't neat today. The women were gathered in the kitchen around the bright jumble of colored scraps. Josefina searched the kitchen with her eyes, hoping to see Niña. There was no doll to be seen, but Josefina couldn't help smiling at the pile of finished ramilletes. It looked as if a flower garden were blooming right there in the middle of Señora Sánchez's kitchen! Josefina turned to Tía Dolores. "The ramilletes remind me of the flowers Mamá planted in our courtyard," she said.

ramillete

22

"Josefina, your mamá would be pleased with the way you've cared for the flowers she planted," said Tía Magdalena, who was Josefina's godmother.

All the women murmured in agreement.

"Things grew well for your mamá," said Señora López.

"Of course they did!" said Señora Sánchez. "And no wonder! She used to say to me, 'You must treat flowers like people!'"

The women nodded and Señor García's wife said, "Well, she certainly treated people kindly. Look how beautifully her daughters are growing." Señora García turned to Tía Dolores. "And you've done well to teach the girls to read and write, and to encourage them to weave."

Tía Dolores smiled. "They've worked very hard," she said.

Josefina felt a warmth that came from more than the fire and the hot, sweet mint tea Señora Sánchez served. She had known these women all her life, as far back as she could remember. They'd helped her when she was a fat-legged toddler always underfoot and falling down just like the toddlers there today. They'd known her when she tagged along watching

Clara and Margarita play dolls, back before Niña disappeared. When Mamá died, all of these women had lost a dear friend. Josefina knew they'd never forget Mamá, any more than she herself would.

"Look!" said Francisca. She held a cloth flower behind one ear. It was made of the yellow material that Tía Dolores had brought. Francisca twitched her skirts and swirled around gracefully as if she were dancing.

Everyone laughed. Ana said, "The flower looks pretty in your hair, Francisca. But it'll look just as pretty in the church on Christmas Eve!"

"We'll put the ramilletes in an arch over the altar," said Señora García to the girls. "And we'll put the cloth your mamá made on the altar."

"Didn't she have a fine hand for *colcha* embroidery?" said Tía Magdalena. "No village in New Mexico has a lovelier Christmas altar cloth."

Señora Sánchez turned to her daughter Margarita, who was going to be María in Las Posadas this year. "Sing for us, Margarita," she said. "Sing the lullaby we always sing on Christmas Eve."

Josefina held her breath while Margarita sang:

Sleep my beautiful baby,
Sleep my grain of gold.

And everyone but Josefina joined in:

The night is very cold,
The night is very cold.

This time, the lullaby didn't make Josefina cry. Instead, as she listened, Josefina thought, *A song like this must go straight up to God like a prayer.*

With all her heart, Josefina wished she had the courage to be María in Las Posadas this Christmas. But with all her heart she was sure that she did not.

The December afternoon was short. The weak winter sun slid down behind the mountains early, and it was nearly dusk when Papá came to walk home with Tía Dolores and the sisters. He had been to the church to get the trunk that had the Christmas altar cloth in it.

Señora Sánchez beckoned to Josefina. "Come with me," she said. "I have something for you and your sisters, to thank you for the chiles."

Josefina followed Señora Sánchez outside. She was very surprised when Señora Sánchez handed her a little cage made out of bent wood. Inside the cage there was the plumpest, prettiest black-and-white hen Josefina had ever seen. "Oh, Señora Sánchez!" Josefina exclaimed. "Gracias!"

Señora Sánchez beamed a generous smile. "She's a vain little hen, very proud of herself, I'm afraid!" she said. "But she has reason to be proud. She lays very fine eggs. I thought you and your sisters could raise her chicks to increase your flock. I know you'll take good care of her."

Josefina thanked Señora Sánchez again. She held up the cage to look at the hen, who puffed herself up and met Josefina's gaze with her beady black eyes. Then Papá strapped the hen's cage onto the burro, next to the trunk from the church. He and Tía Dolores and the sisters began the long walk home.

"Adiós!" the women called out after them. "God keep you well!"

Josefina turned and waved. "Adiós!" she called.

It had been a long, full day and Josefina was tired. As she walked along next to Clara she said happily, "The ramilletes we made will look beautiful in the church, won't they?"

"I suppose so," said Clara, rather sourly. "Of

Papá strapped the hen's cage onto the burro.

course, no one will know how to arrange them as nicely as Mamá used to." She sighed. "Oh, well, at least the altar cloth will look all right. *It* will be the way it used to be."

When they were home at the rancho, Papá carried the trunk into the kitchen and set it down near the fire. "Wait till you see Mamá's altar cloth," Josefina said to Tía Dolores. "The birds that Mamá embroidered on it look so real you expect them to sing!"

Tía Dolores smiled. She knelt next to the trunk. Papá and all the sisters crowded around, peering over her shoulders as she lifted the lid. Tía Dolores lifted the altar cloth out of the trunk and they all looked at it. For a moment, no one said anything. Then Papá pulled his breath in sharply, as if something had hurt him. Without a word, he turned and left the room.

Josefina was confused. What was this torn, bedraggled cloth in Tía Dolores's hands? This cloth looked like a rag. It was chewed by mice. It smelled of mildew. It was water-stained and dirty. It couldn't

be Mamá's beautiful embroidered altar cloth.
But it was.

"Oh, no," said Ana, sounding miserable. "Water from the flood must have rotted the leather of the trunk so that mice and dampness got in. Just look at the damage that's been done."

"It's *ruined!*" Clara cried out. "It's ruined, just like Christmas!" She rushed from the room.

The door slammed behind her, and the whole room and everyone in it was shaken. It wasn't like Clara to act like that. Her words echoed in Josefina's head: *It's ruined, just like Christmas . . .* The knot inside Josefina tightened again. Just when Josefina had begun to hope that this Christmas might be happy, *this* had to happen. The beautiful altar cloth Mamá had made so lovingly was destroyed. It hurt Josefina to look at it on Tía Dolores's lap.

Tía Dolores unfolded the altar cloth slowly, never minding the dirt and mildew that soiled her skirt. The more she unfolded it, the more damage Josefina saw.

Francisca lifted one corner, using just the tips of her fingers. "Just look!" she said. "It's in shreds!"

Ana sighed. "I'm glad Mamá is not here to see

this," she said. "It would break her heart."

Tía Dolores didn't say anything. She examined the cloth carefully, running her hands over it. Then she said, "I think we can repair this."

Ana, Francisca, and Josefina looked at each other. "But how?" asked Francisca.

"First, we'll wash it," said Tía Dolores. "Then we'll iron it. We'll mend the embroidery wherever we can."

"But what about the embroidery that the mice chewed away?" asked Ana.

"We'll replace it with new embroidery," said Tía Dolores.

Francisca looked doubtful. "We'll need Clara for that," she said. "Mamá taught us all colcha embroidery, but Clara's the best. She's the only one who's even close to doing colcha as well as Mamá."

"Very well," said Tía Dolores. "Josefina, please go to Clara and ask her to come back so that I may speak to her."

Josefina nodded. Quickly, she crossed the courtyard to the room she shared with Francisca and Clara. The door was partly open, and through it Josefina heard the sound of Clara crying. Josefina stood still, not sure what to do. As she hesitated, she looked into the room. It was dark, but Josefina saw Clara open the clothes trunk and take out an old skirt that was neatly folded into a thick bundle. Clara unfolded the skirt. Josefina saw a bit of something pale blue, a flash of green, *and there was Niña!*

Josefina gasped in surprise and bewilderment. Clara had Niña! The doll had been hidden in Clara's trunk all this time! Josefina took one step into the room, then stopped short when she saw Clara bury her face in Niña and sob. Clara cried as if her heart were broken, and she held on to Niña as if the doll were her only comfort in the world. Josefina turned away quietly so that Clara wouldn't hear her.

When Josefina got back to the kitchen, Ana and Francisca were gone. Tía Dolores was alone, still holding the altar cloth.

"Is Clara coming?" asked Tía Dolores.

"I . . . I don't know," stammered Josefina.

Tía Dolores looked confused. She asked, "Didn't you speak to her?"

"No," said Josefina. Suddenly, she burst out, "Tía Dolores, Clara has Niña! I saw her! The door was open a little and when I looked in, I saw Clara holding the doll!" Josefina spoke as if she could hardly believe what she had seen. "Clara has known where Niña is all along. She's been keeping her for herself!"

Tía Dolores put the altar cloth down and took both Josefina's hands in her own. "I'm not sure I understand it," she said slowly. "But I think Clara misses your mamá very, very much. Your mamá made Niña, and she made a new dress for her every Christmas. So Niña is a way for Clara to feel close to your mamá. She's a comfort. Clara needs her."

"But why did she pretend she didn't know where Niña was?" asked Josefina indignantly. "That wasn't *true*."

"Do you remember the other day when you told me how you're not ready to be María in Las Posadas?" Tía Dolores asked.

Josefina nodded.

"Well, Clara is not ready to give you Niña. That's why she's hiding her," said Tía Dolores. She looked at Josefina's long face and tried to cheer her. "At least we know that Niña isn't lost. She's safe. That's good, isn't it?"

"I guess so," Josefina admitted grudgingly. "But when will Clara give her to me? Will Niña ever be mine?"

Tía Dolores sighed. "I don't know," she said. "No one knows, probably not even Clara. It may take a long time." She put Josefina's hands aside and picked up the altar cloth again. "Just as it'll take time to repair this altar cloth. But we'll do it. The sooner we begin, the better." Tía Dolores tried to tease a smile out of Josefina. "What do I always say?" she asked.

Josefina had to smile just a little bit, in spite of Clara, in spite of Niña, and in spite of herself. "You always say, 'The saints cry over lost time.'"

"Precisely!" said Tía Dolores briskly. "We'll start tomorrow!"

THE SILVER THIMBLE

And they did start repairing the altar cloth the very next day—everyone except Clara. Josefina helped Tía Dolores wash the altar cloth in warm, soapy water and rinse it in clear, cool water. Gently, Tía Dolores wrung out the cloth. Then she and Josefina spread it to dry in a sunny corner of the back courtyard. When the cloth was dry, Ana ironed it smooth, being careful not to scorch it with the hot irons heated by the fire. Francisca helped Josefina mend some of the holes the mice had chewed, and Tía Dolores cut off the end where the holes were too big to mend. She attached a new piece of material in its place.

At last the time came to begin the colcha

embroidery. Tía Dolores and the four sisters gathered in front of the fire as they did every evening. Tía Dolores spread out the altar cloth. "What shall we embroider?" she asked, looking at the sisters.

Josefina looked at the altar cloth. Firelight brightened the colors of the designs that Mamá had stitched. Josefina had an idea. "Wait," she said. Very quickly, she went to her room and found her memory box, the little box in which she kept things that reminded her of Mamá. She brought the box back to the fireside. "Mamá made the altar cloth," she said. "I think we should embroider things on it that she loved. Maybe the things in my box will give us ideas."

Josefina opened her memory box, and Francisca took a swallow's feather out of it. "Mamá loved swallows," Francisca said. "I'll embroider swallows and other birds on the altar cloth."

Ana took a bit of lavender-scented soap out of the box. She smelled it. "I'll stitch sprigs of lavender," she said. "Mamá loved its scent."

"And I'll embroider leaves and flowers," said Josefina as she took a dried primrose out of her memory box. "Because Mamá loved them."

"And what will you embroider, Clara?" Tía Dolores asked.

Clara was only halfway in the firelight. She looked at the altar cloth with critical eyes. "It doesn't matter," she said. "We can't make that cloth look right again without Mamá anyway."

"We can," said Tía Dolores firmly. "It'll take time, but we can repair it. And if we all work together, I think we'll even enjoy doing it."

Clara drew back out of the light, but Josefina saw her face. It looked as sad as it did in the moment Josefina had seen Clara holding Niña and crying. Suddenly, Josefina felt sorry for Clara. "Doing the colcha embroidery makes me miss Mamá, too, Clara," Josefina said. "It makes her seem very far away, doesn't it?"

Clara didn't answer.

"Perhaps this will help," said Tía Dolores. She reached in her pocket and took out a silver thimble. "Your mamá gave this to me a long time ago when we were girls. She was trying to teach me how to do colcha. I didn't like it because I kept pricking myself with the needle and it hurt. She gave me the thimble to protect my finger.

36

Now all of you may use it to protect *your* fingers."

Clara leaned forward on her stool. She looked at the thimble and then at Tía Dolores. "If Mamá gave something like that to me, I'd keep it forever," she said. "I wouldn't dream of giving it away!"

Just like Niña, thought Josefina with a heavy heart.

"But it makes me happy to share the thimble," said Tía Dolores. "When we use it, we'll think of your mamá with every stitch we make. Perhaps it will make her seem closer, not farther away."

"Oh, please, may I use it?" Josefina asked.

Tía Dolores handed the silver thimble to Josefina and she put it on her finger. It looked shiny in the light of the fire. As she began stitching, Josefina used the thimble to help push the needle through the cloth. She knew Clara was watching her. When Josefina started to tie a knot at the end of the wool she was using, Clara moved next to her.

"Don't," said Clara. "Have you forgotten? Mamá said never to knot the wool. Use your second stitch to hold your first stitch in place. Here, let me show you. I'll stitch the stem of that flower for you."

Clara spread the cloth over her knees and

took the needle from Josefina. She began to stitch. Francisca nudged Ana, and Ana raised her eyebrows at Josefina as if to say, *This is a surprise!*

Josefina took the thimble off her finger. "Use this," she said.

Clara stopped for a moment and looked at the thimble. Then, slowly, she took it from Josefina and slipped it on her own finger. "Gracias," she said, but so quietly only Josefina could hear her.

Josefina gave herself the job of untangling knots in the wool Tía Dolores was using. When she looked up a little while later, Josefina saw that Clara had finished stitching the stem and was embroidering a yellow blossom on the end of it. Josefina saw that Clara's stitches were smooth and sure and secure.

She also saw that Clara hadn't taken the silver thimble off her finger.

On a still, cold evening a few days later, Tía Dolores and the sisters were working on the altar cloth in front of the fire. "Francisca," said Josefina. "That chicken you're stitching looks just like the pretty little hen that Señora Sánchez gave us."

Francisca groaned and pretended to be annoyed. "It's not supposed to be a chicken," she said. "It's supposed to be a sparrow!" She held the altar cloth up so that Tía Dolores, Ana, and Clara could see it, too. "What do you think?" she asked. "Can we pretend that it's a very fat sparrow?"

"One that clucks instead of singing?" teased Josefina.

They all laughed, and Clara said, "I can fix it for you. It just needs its feathers smoothed a bit."

"Gracias!" said Francisca. She let Clara take her needle with relief.

Ana had been wearing the silver thimble, but now she handed it to Clara. "You'll need this," she joked. "Francisca's chicken might peck at you!"

Tía Dolores was right, thought Josefina as they all laughed again. *We are enjoying working together to repair Mamá's altar cloth.*

"I remember when Mamá taught me to do colcha," said Clara. "She told me, 'You'll like colcha. You have hands that need to be busy.'" Tía Dolores and the sisters smiled at Clara's memory. Josefina watched Clara stitch and admired, as she always did, the way the silver thimble shone in the firelight.

The four sisters and Tía Dolores worked on the cloth almost every evening, and it was a time Josefina looked forward to. They took turns wearing the silver thimble. Francisca made a game out of it. She said that whoever wore the thimble had to share a memory about Mamá. Sometimes the memories would make Josefina sad. But sometimes they made her laugh because they reminded her of happy times. Just as the thimble protected Josefina and her sisters from the pain of being pricked by the needle, it seemed also to protect them from the pain that memories of Mamá used to bring.

Repairing the altar cloth was slow work. But as the days went by, stitch by stitch the cloth became beautiful again. And as the days went by, bit by bit Josefina began to feel better about all the things this Christmas might bring—even though she was now quite sure Niña was *not* going to be one of them.

Before they knew it, Christmas was only nine days away, and it was time for Las Posadas to begin. On the first night of Las Posadas, it was snowing lightly when Josefina and her family walked to the village. Papá led the way, holding a lantern high to light the road. When they came into the plaza, Josefina could see hot orange sparks from the bonfires rising up to meet the cold white snowflakes. The biggest bonfire was in front of the church. Almost all their friends and neighbors and all the workers from Papá's rancho had gathered around it. Everyone greeted the Montoyas when they joined the circle, and their breath puffed clouds into the sharp air. As Josefina watched Margarita Sánchez climb onto the burro and settle her skirts around her, she thought Margarita would be a very fine María. Because it was the village tradition, Margarita's papá was being José. He led the burro to the first house and everyone followed. He knocked on the door, and they all sang:

In heaven's name, we ask for shelter.

And the people inside sang back:

This is not an inn! Be on your way!

At first, Josefina didn't even try to join the singing. She hung back, expecting to feel the same heavy, ice-cold weight of sorrow she'd felt last year. Back then, she had missed the sound of Mamá's voice so much that the music had been painful to hear. But tonight, the music wasn't painful. It sounded gentle and familiar. Josefina listened very hard. It seemed to her that the music helped her remember the sound of Mamá's voice, and so she was glad to hear it. Josefina looked at the faces that surrounded her. She saw Señor García's thin, kindly old face and Margarita Sánchez's young, round face. She saw Ana, Francisca, and Clara with snowflakes clinging to their hair. She heard Papá's voice, so low she could feel it inside her,

Tonight, the music wasn't painful. It sounded gentle and familiar.

and Tía Dolores's voice, strong and clear. It was a comfort to be surrounded by these good people who had loved Mamá too. *Oh, Mamá,* Josefina thought. *We all miss you so much!* Somehow, the thought made missing Mamá easier to bear.

Josefina shivered. But it was the beautiful music that made her shiver, not cold or sorrow. As she listened, Josefina thought about how people had been singing these same songs at Las Posadas for hundreds of years. They sang to honor God and to remember the first Christmas when Jesús was born. Josefina thought back to when Mamá taught *her* the songs so that she could join in the tradition. She remembered all the Christmases when she and Mamá had taken part in Las Posadas together, and the memories were both sad and sweet.

Tonight, the last house the procession went to was the Sánchez family's house. This time, after the people outside asked for shelter, the people inside opened the door wide. Josefina saw Señora Sánchez's good-natured face in the doorway and heard her sing louder than anyone else:

Come in, weary travelers. You are welcome!

Josefina grinned. No one could doubt that
Señora Sánchez truly meant the welcoming words
from her heart! And Josefina meant it, too, when she
and the others sang their thanks in return:

> *God bless you for your kindness,*
> *And may heaven fill you with peace and joy!*

Then everyone crowded inside for prayers and
more singing before the party began. In the
Sánchez family's house, the air was spicy
with the delicious aroma of meat pies and
tamales and, of course, Señora Sánchez's
famous stew. Josefina saw Clara and
Margarita warming themselves by the fire.

meat pies and tamales

They were looking at the ramilletes, and Clara was
holding up a scrap of yellow cloth as if she were
planning to make more flowers. Her face looked
happy and eager.

Josefina thought that Clara must be feeling the
same way she was—as if a heavy burden had started
to slip away.

LA NOCHE BUENA

Every day was colder than the one before, and Christmas Eve day was bone-chilling. The sky was dark as stone from dawn till dusk, and sleet fell without stopping. Josefina's hands were stiff as she and Clara put the final stitches in the altar cloth late that afternoon.

At last the cloth was finished. Tía Dolores held one end and Ana held the other so that they could fold it carefully. One of the flowers Clara had embroidered ended up on top. Tía Dolores stroked the flower gently. "Clara," she said. "You have your mamá's gift for embroidery. Truly you do."

"I can't tell Clara's flowers from those Mamá made," agreed Ana.

A quick, pleased smile lit Clara's face. She took the silver thimble off her finger and held it out to Tía Dolores. "Thank you for sharing this with us," she said.

Tía Dolores didn't take the thimble. Instead she said, "Perhaps Josefina will let us keep it in her memory box. It'll be handy there."

"Sí," said Josefina. "Go ahead, Clara. You can put the thimble in the box. It's on the shelf in our room."

But Clara put the thimble in the palm of Josefina's hand and then curled Josefina's fingers around it so that it was held tight in her fist. "No," Clara said. "I think you should go and put it in your memory box, Josefina."

"Sí, put it safely away," said Tía Dolores. "And Clara, you'd better go, too. It's time for you girls to change your clothes." She smiled. "It's Christmas Eve!"

Josefina and Clara hurried across the courtyard to their room. Francisca, who shared the room with them, had finished dressing. She'd left a small candle in the room to give Clara and Josefina light to dress by. But as they came in, it seemed to

Josefina that the room was illuminated by more than one single candle. Josefina smiled when she saw why. Someone had laid out Josefina's *mantilla,* comb, and best dress on top of the trunk. The pretty yellow dress brightened the whole room. Josefina walked toward it, then stopped, stared, and gasped in surprise. For there, sitting on top of her yellow dress, was Niña!

mantilla and comb

Josefina lifted Niña up. She saw that Niña's face looked just as she remembered it. The eyes Mamá had sewn out of black thread still looked lively, and the mouth Mamá had sewn out of pink thread still smiled sweetly. Niña's yarn hair was smooth and untangled. Her arms and legs were plump with new stuffing. Best of all, Niña had a new yellow dress that exactly matched Josefina's. It had a long skirt and long sleeves gathered in puffs up near the shoulders. Niña even had a tiny new mantilla like Josefina's, and pantalettes and a petticoat. Josefina hugged Niña and kissed her soft cheeks.

"She's yours," said Clara.

"Oh, Clara!" Josefina whispered. "Gracias!"

She hugged Niña closer. "I thought she never would be."

"Why not?" asked Clara.

"I . . . I knew that you had her," Josefina admitted, "and I—"

"You knew?" interrupted Clara.

"Sí," answered Josefina.

"Why didn't you say anything?" Clara asked.

"Well," said Josefina, "Tía Dolores told me that you needed her."

Very slowly, Clara nodded. "I did need her," she said. "I thought she was all I had left from

Mamá. But now I know that I have Mamá's gift for embroidery, and I'll never lose that."

Josefina touched the smooth ribbon around the high waist of Niña's dress. "Did you make this dress for Niña?" Josefina asked.

"Sí," said Clara. "I wanted to carry on the tradition that Mamá started."

Josefina smiled broadly at Clara. "Niña's dress is beautiful," she said. "I think maybe you have Mamá's gift for making doll dresses, too!"

Clara smiled back. Then she looked lovingly at Niña. "I went to Niña for comfort because I thought I had nowhere else to go," she said. "But now I know that there's comfort all around me if I need it."

"Sí," said Josefina. "I'm finding that out also." She opened her fist, and the silver thimble shone in the candlelight. "I'll put the thimble in my memory box so that we can share it," Josefina said to Clara. "And we'll share Niña, too. She'll sleep between us from now on."

Christmas Eve was called *la Noche buena*—the good night. And this Christmas Eve felt like a very good night to Josefina. Niña was hers to love and care for at last. The weather was still sleety and cold, so Josefina wore a rebozo crisscrossed over her chest and tied behind her waist under the outer blanket she wore for warmth. She tucked Niña inside her rebozo and held her tight as she and her family walked to the village. It was later than usual, because tonight Las Posadas would end at the church and the priest, Padre Simón, would begin Mass at the stroke of midnight. After Mass, everyone would stream out of the church into the frosty blackness and wish each other *feliz Navidad*—happy Christmas. Then there was going to be a party at the Garcías' house. Josefina knew there would be music and dancing and a wonderful feast. Ana was bringing a silver tray piled high with sweet bizcochito cookies like Mamá used to make. Josefina hugged Niña in happy anticipation of it all.

A big bonfire glowed gold in the darkness in front of the church. Josefina was glad to see it. She was glad to go inside the church, too, where it was dry. Sleet had beaded her blanket as if it were covered with thousands of tiny pearls. Josefina took the blanket off and shook it just inside the door of the church. She checked to be sure that Niña was held safe in her rebozo, then hurried to catch up with Papá and Tía Dolores and her sisters. They were near the altar with Señor García and other friends and neighbors who had come to decorate the church.

Tía Dolores gave the altar cloth to Señor García.

"Gracias, gracias!" said Señor García to Tía Dolores and the sisters. "I am told that all of you had to work hard to repair this. God bless you!"

"Everyone is grateful," added Señora López. "Now our altar will be as beautiful as it has been in years past."

"Padre Simón is on his way," said Señor García. "Some men from the village have gone to greet him and lead him to the church. Perhaps we had better begin to decorate. Soon it will be time to start Las Posadas."

Only a few candles were lit. Most were being saved for when Padre Simón would say Mass. The church was shadowy, and Josefina felt as if she and the others who quietly set about decorating were preparing a lovely surprise. Josefina helped Papá and Señor López arrange pine branches around the little wooden stable that was part of the Nativity scene. The branches smelled fresh with the tang of mountain air. Then Josefina helped put the carved wooden figures from the Nativity scene in their places. She helped spread the cloth on the altar and smooth out any wrinkles. Ana and Francisca and a group of girls had just finished arranging the colorful ramilletes in an arch over the altar when Señora Sánchez hurried into the church. She looked distressed.

"Pardon me, Señor García," she said breathlessly. "I'm afraid I have bad news. My daughter Margarita is ill. She must have caught a cold from being outside on these bitter nights. She is too ill to be María tonight. She can't stir from her bed!"

"Poor Margarita!" said Señor García.

Everyone dropped what they were doing and gathered around Señora Sánchez and Señor García. They shook their heads and murmured, "Oh, the poor child! Bless her soul!"

Josefina's heart beat fast. She asked herself a question, and thought hard about the answer.

Slipping one hand inside her rebozo so that it was touching Niña, Josefina used the other hand to tug gently on Señor García's sleeve.

Señor García turned to her. Josefina's voice was small but steady as she looked up at him and said, "Please, Señor García, may I be María?" Everyone looked at Josefina as she went on, "I'd like to pray that this will be a happy Christmas for us and for my mamá in heaven."

Señor García's thin old face was solemn. Slowly, he nodded. "Sí, my child," he said to Josefina. "You may be María."

Josefina turned to Papá. "Will you be José?" she asked him.

"I will," said Papá gravely. He didn't smile, but he looked at Josefina with pride and love.

Tía Dolores did, too.

When it was time, Josefina handed Niña to Clara for safekeeping. "Please hold her for me," Josefina said. "Keep her warm."

Clara took the doll. "I will," she promised.

They all went outside. The wind was blowing

hard, driving the sleet so that it stung Josefina's face. Papá lifted Josefina up onto the burro's back. She knew Señor Sánchez's burro was gentle. But still, she felt very high off the ground. Josefina was glad Papá would be walking at her side leading the burro. She took the reins and held on tight.

A gust of wind made the skirt of her dress flutter. Papá was wearing an extra blanket over his *sarape*. He took it off now and said, "You'd better wear this over your own blanket. It'll keep you warm."

"Gracias," said Josefina as Papá wrapped her in the blanket. It covered her from head to foot.

As the villagers gathered to begin the procession, many people stopped to speak to Papá and Josefina. Gently, they touched Papá's shoulder or Josefina's foot or the end of the blanket Papá had wrapped around her. "May God grant you a good and long life," they said.

Josefina tried to sit up as straight as she could on the burro's back. Then, with a slow *clop clop* of the burro's hooves on the frozen ground, they moved to the first house. Papá knocked on the door, and they all sang:

In heaven's name, we ask for shelter.

And the people inside sang back:

This is not an inn! Be on your way!

Josefina's voice was unsteady at first. She felt nervous and stiff because she was self-conscious. But, as they had on every other night, the lovely music and words soon made Josefina forget all about herself and her shyness. After a while, Josefina was singing the Las Posadas songs in a voice that was full of all the hope and happiness of Christmas.

Papá led the burro from house to house. At each house, he and Josefina and everyone with them sang, asking for shelter. And at each house, the people inside sang back, telling them to go away. Then everyone inside the house came out to join the group behind Papá. After the last house, Papá turned back to the church. By that time, everyone in the whole village and all the workers from the rancho were in the crowd. Josefina felt as if everyone she knew and loved in the world were there behind her.

When they got to the church, Papá knocked on the doors. *Boom! Boom! Boom!* The sound echoed inside. Then everyone sang:

María, Queen of Heaven, begs for shelter
For just one night, kind sir!

Padre Simón opened one of the church doors just a bit. He looked out and sang:

Come in, weary travelers. You are welcome!

Then Padre Simón flung both doors open wide. Golden candlelight flooded out. The church bell rang. And everyone sang:

God bless you for your kindness,
And may heaven fill you with peace and joy!

Papá lifted Josefina down off the burro. She was glad for his strong arms, because her legs felt wobbly and numb from the cold. The big blanket Papá had wrapped around her was weighted down with a coating of sleet, but when she took it off, her own blanket underneath it was dry.

"Josefina," she heard someone whisper. It was Clara, who handed Niña to her. Josefina tucked Niña safe inside her rebozo again. Then Tía Dolores took Josefina by one hand and Papá took the other, and

Padre Simón looked out and sang, "Come in, weary travelers.
You are welcome!"

they walked into the church behind Padre Simón. Ana, Francisca, Clara, and everyone else followed.

Josefina could hardly breathe. The church was so beautiful, she felt as if she were walking into a dream. All the candles were lit. Their brightness made the candlesticks shine and the polished wood glow. The candles cast a warm light on the Nativity scene in its nest of pine branches and on the delicate ramilletes arched gracefully above the altar.

But to Josefina, the most beautiful thing by far was Mamá's altar cloth. Perhaps it was because she knew and loved every stitch of it after working on it for so long with Tía Dolores and her sisters. In the wavering candlelight, the soft, flowing leaves and flowers seemed to be floating in a gentle breeze, and the colors were rich and true. Josefina looked at the newly embroidered flowers with pride. *Mamá would be pleased,* she thought.

By now the church was full of people, and Padre Simón began the Mass. When it was time for her to sing the beginning of the lullaby, Josefina stood up, closed her eyes, and sang:

Sleep my beautiful baby,
Sleep my grain of gold.

Her voice was the only sound in the church, like a bird singing all alone on a mountaintop. Then Josefina opened her eyes, and everyone sang with her:

The night is very cold,
The night is very cold.

Josefina listened to all the voices soaring up around her, and she felt as safe and as loved as she used to feel when Mamá sang the lullaby to her.

Josefina hugged Niña close, sure that her prayer for a happy Christmas had been answered.

A PEEK INTO
THE PAST

For New Mexicans, Christmas was a holy time, and the church was an important part of their celebrations. This village church was built about the time Josefina was born.

When winter came to the mountains of New Mexico, everyone began to look forward to Christmas, or *Navidad*. In Josefina's time, the Christmas season lasted nearly a month. It was a time for people to celebrate their faith, give thanks for their blessings, and enjoy evenings filled with delicious food, music, dancing, and the company of friends and relatives.

The Christmas season began in early December. People decorated their homes and the village church with Nativity scenes, pine boughs,

This Nativity scene was made in New Mexico in the late 1700s. It shows Joseph, Mary, and baby Jesus on the first Christmas.

and handmade flowers. As Christmas neared, women and girls started cooking holiday treats such as spicy stews, *tamales*, and cookies called *bizcochitos*.

Religious plays were part of the Christmas season, too—just as they had been for hundreds of years in Spain and Mexico. They usually combined religious stories with music and some humorous scenes. In a time when many people could not read, plays were a way for people to enjoy themselves and to keep their religious beliefs alive.

One play, called *Las Posadas* or "The Inns," was performed throughout New Mexico at Christmastime, just as it was in Josefina's village. For nine nights in a row, beginning on December 16, each village acted out the story of Jesus' parents searching for lodging on the first Christmas Eve in Bethlehem. The two people playing the roles of Mary and Joseph—or María and José in Spanish—went from house to house, asking for a place to stay. Villagers followed behind them, holding candles and singing

*Spanish settlers carried the Christmas tradition of **Las Posadas** to many parts of the world. This engraving shows a Las Posadas procession in Mexico City in the mid-1800s.*

hymns. Their way was lit by bonfires called *luminarias.*
At every house they were turned away, just as Mary and
Joseph were. Finally, at the last house they were welcomed, and the whole village was invited inside for music, dancing, and treats such as hot chocolate and sweets. Performing the role of Mary or Joseph was an important

Music, dancing, and warm hospitality were all important parts of Christmas celebrations.

Chocolate pot, cup, and stirrer

responsibility. Las Posadas was a kind of prayer, and often the people who played Mary and Joseph were praying for something special, just as Josefina was when she played Mary.

The biggest celebration took place on *la Noche buena,* or Christmas Eve. In the early evening, villagers gathered for singing, prayers, storytelling, and music played on guitars and fiddles.

A handmade fiddle from the 1800s

Then the last performance of Las Posadas began. On this night, Las Posadas ended at the church. Few villages had their own priest in 1824. If a priest was available, he performed the beautiful Christmas church service of Midnight Mass. If there was no priest, people gathered in the church to pray, sing hymns, and perform a Christmas play called *Los Pastores*, or "The Shepherds." Afterward, there were parties and feasts until dawn. Children loved la Noche buena because they got to stay up all night enjoying the festivities and listening to stories and songs.

Both children and adults had roles in Christmas plays.

*The Christmas play called **Los Pastores** has been performed in New Mexico for hundreds of years. In this photo, taken about 1915, a boy is playing the part of the archangel Michael. He is fighting against the devil, who is shown at left wearing horns.*

For centuries, many Pueblo Indian villages have held special dances at Christmastime. One of the most common is the Deer Dance, shown in the photo above. The engraving at left shows a Pueblo ceremonial dance in the 1850s.

The Pueblo Indian villages of New Mexico celebrated Christmas, too. The settlers often visited a nearby Pueblo village to watch the Christmas dances. Almost everyone in the Pueblo village would take part in the dances, which were usually performed to the slow, steady beating of drums and lasted most of the day. Afterward, visitors like Josefina's family would be welcomed into the homes of the Pueblo people to share a festive meal.

The Christmas season ended on January 6, the Feast of the Three Kings. The night before, children left straw

These handmade statues illustrate the Bible story of the three kings, who followed a bright star to bring gifts to the baby Jesus.

in their shoes to feed the camels of
the three kings, and in the morning
they found that the straw had been replaced
by sweets or small toys!

Today, New Mexican children still love traditions
such as Las Posadas, Midnight Mass, and Pueblo dances.
Children enjoy spicy stews, tamales, and bizcochito
cookies, just as Josefina did. But instead of lighting
Christmas bonfires, New Mexicans today
set out small lights called *farolitos*, made
of candles set securely inside paper bags.
All these traditions, old and new, make
Christmas in New Mexico as magical
today as it was in Josefina's time.

*The glowing lights of **farolitos** are a favorite New Mexican Christmas tradition today.
Above, a modern-day girl plays the role of María in Las Posadas.*

Glossary of Spanish Words

adiós *(ah-dee-OHS)*—good-bye

adobe *(ah-DOH-beh)*—a building material made of earth mixed with straw and water. Most New Mexican houses were built of adobe.

bizcochito *(bees-ko-CHEE-toh)*—a kind of sugar cookie flavored with anise

buenos días *(BWEH-nohs DEE-ahs)*—good morning

colcha *(KOHL-chah)*—a kind of embroidery made with long, flat stitches

farolito *(fah-ro-LEE-toh)*—a decoration made by placing a candle securely in a brown paper bag, so its light shines through the paper and gives off a golden glow

feliz Navidad *(feh-LEES nah-vee-DAHD)*—merry Christmas

gracias *(GRAH-see-ahs)*—thank you

la Noche buena *(lah NO-cheh BWEH-nah)*—Christmas Eve. The Spanish words mean "the good night."

Las Posadas *(lahs po-SAH-dahs)*—a religious drama that acts out the story of the first Christmas Eve. Its name means "The Inns."

Los Pastores *(lohs pahs-TOH-res)*—a Christmas play that tells how an angel announced Jesus' birth to shepherds nearby. Its name means "The Shepherds."

luminaria *(loo-mee-NAH-ree-ah)*—a small bonfire to give light and cheer for celebrations

mantilla *(mahn-TEE-yah)*—a lacy scarf that girls and women wear over their head and shoulders

mayordomo *(mah-yor-DOH-mo)*—a man who is elected to take charge of town or church affairs

Navidad *(nah-vee-DAHD)*—Christmas

Padre *(PAH-dreh)*—the title for a priest. It means "Father."

piñón *(pee-NYOHN)*—a kind of short, scrubby pine tree

plaza *(PLAH-sah)*—an open square in a village or town

ramillete *(rah-mee-YEH-teh)*—a branch or bouquet of flowers used for decoration

rancho *(RAHN-cho)*—a farm or ranch where crops are grown and animals are raised

rebozo *(reh-BO-so)*—a long shawl worn by girls and women

sala *(SAH-lah)*—a large room in a house

sarape *(sah-RAH-peh)*—a warm blanket that is wrapped around the shoulders or worn as a poncho

Señor *(seh-NYOR)*—Mr.

Señora *(seh-NYO-rah)*—Mrs.

sí *(SEE)*—yes

tamales *(tah-MAH-les)*—spicy meat surrounded by cornmeal dough and cooked in a cornhusk wrapping

tía *(TEE-ah)*—aunt

THE AMERICAN GIRLS COLLECTION®

FELICITY   JOSEFINA   KIRSTEN   ADDY   SAMANTHA   MOLLY

There are more books in The American Girls Collection. They're filled with the adventures that six lively American girls lived long ago.

The books are the heart of The American Girls Collection, but they are only the beginning. There are also lovable dolls that have beautiful clothes and lots of wonderful accessories. They make these stories of the past come alive today for American girls like you.

To learn about The American Girls Collection, fill out this postcard and mail it to Pleasant Company, or call **1-800-845-0005**. We will send you a catalogue about all the books, dolls, dresses, and other delights in The American Girls Collection.

I'm an American girl who loves to get mail. Please send me a catalogue of The American Girls Collection:

My name is _____

My address is _____

City_____ State _____ Zip_____

Parent's signature _____

1961

And send a catalogue to my friend:

My friend's name is _____

Address _____

City_____ State _____ Zip_____

1225

The AMERICAN GIRLS CLUB™

Do you love the American Girls? Then join the Club—The American Girls Club! It's for girls like you to discover even more about Felicity, Josefina, Kirsten, Addy, Samantha, and Molly. Meet fellow Club members through the Club newspaper, *The American Girls News*™—it's like having a Club meeting in your home six times a year! As a member, you'll also receive a Club handbook bursting with crafts, projects, and activities to last the whole year! For a free catalogue full of exciting Club details, fill out the attached card or call us today!

Join the Club fun! Call 1-800-845-0005 today!